Serge –

THIS WALKER BOOK BELONGS TO:

_____

_____

_____

_____

I hope

day –

Best wishes!

Elisabeth Beresford.

ALDERNEY 1994.

# The Invisible Wombles
## and other stories

It was while walking on Wimbledon Common with her two children that Elisabeth Beresford had the idea for the Wombles. But when the first book in the series appeared in 1968, she had already written over twenty-five other children's books – mainly stories of adventure or magic.

The Wombles, she hoped, would 'make children want to fight pollution and to think up ways of "making good use of bad rubbish"(the Womble family motto).' Over the years the exploits of her delightfully tidy characters have done just that – and their lasting popularity has seen them chosen as the mascots for the Tidy Britain campaign.

Written to 'make readers of all ages laugh', these stories about Great Uncle Bulgaria, Tobermory, Orinoco, Bungo, Tomsk, Wellington and the rest have been read and loved by children (and adults) the world over. Many have also watched and enjoyed the Wombles' programmes on television. Quite a few have even bought their records, such as 'Remember You're a Womble'. All of which proves that the Wombles are among the very favourite children's characters ever. So, if you haven't read any of their books before, you're in for a real treat now!

Elisabeth Beresford is also the author of several adult novels and plays. She lives in the Channel Islands.

Also by Elisabeth Beresford

*The Wombles*
*The Wandering Wombles*
*The Wombles at Work*
*The Wombles to the Rescue*

# The Invisible Womble
# and Other Stories

## Elisabeth Beresford

*Illustrated by*
*Ivor Wood*

WALKER BOOKS
LONDON

First published 1973 by Ernest Benn Limited
This edition published 1990 by Walker Books Ltd
87 Vauxhall Walk, London SE11 5HJ

Text © 1973 Elisabeth Beresford
Cover illustrations © 1990 Edgar Hodges
Illustrations based on original film puppet designs
by Ivor Wood © 1973 FilmFair

Printed and bound in Great Britain by
Richard Clay Ltd, Bungay, Suffolk

British Library Cataloguing in Publication Data
Beresford, Elisabeth
The invisible Womble and other stories.
I. Title
823'.914 [F]
ISBN 0-7445-1747-8

# Contents

# Introduction

The Wombles are the tidiest creatures in the world. Every day small groups of working Wombles go round clearing up the rubbish which has been left behind by people, and as they are very clever with their paws they often turn this rubbish into all kinds of useful things. They live in large and extremely comfortable and cosy burrows under the ground, and this particular book is about the Wombles whose home is underneath Wimbledon Common.*

The Womble-in-Charge of this burrow is GREAT UNCLE BULGARIA. He is very

*In The Wandering Wombles and The Wombles at Work they had moved to a burrow under Hyde Park because ... but that's another story!

old indeed and his fur has turned snow white with age, and because his eyes aren't quite as sharp as they used to be he has two pairs of spectacles. He feels the cold a bit too these days so he wears a MacWomble tartan shawl. Great Uncle Bulgaria can be rather strict at times, but he has a very kind heart and he's very wise. The young Wombles believe that he knows everything. Great Uncle Bulgaria sometimes thinks he does too.

Next in age comes TOBERMORY whose fur has turned a silky grey. He's in charge of the Workshop, where he makes all kinds of remarkable and useful gadgets out of the rubbish which the working Wombles bring to him. He and Great Uncle Bulgaria are firm friends and they often shake their wise old heads about some of the rather silly things that young Wombles get up to.

The Womble they shake their heads about

most is BUNGO. Bungo *is* rather inclined to be bossy and self-important, but he's all right really and his best friends are, first of all, ORINOCO.

Orinoco is just about the fattest (which is very fat indeed as all the Wombles have nice round figures) and laziest Womble in the burrow. He quite often needs 'a little forty winks' before he can get his strength up to start work.

Next comes TOMSK. He is the largest of all the Wimbledon Wombles and he finds thinking

rather difficult, but he's wonderful at games and is very keen on keeping fit. He often tries to get Orinoco to take a bit more exercise, but he hasn't succeeded so far. Finally there's WELLINGTON

who is the smallest and shyest working Womble. He wears spectacles and is rather absent-minded (he gets teased about this), but on the other hand he gets all kinds of clever ideas, such as the first-ever-keep-in-touch-Womble-telephone.

And then there is MADAME CHOLET the

cook. She produces the most delicious meals out of all kinds of strange things. Her elm-bark pie with fluffy toadstool topping is famous throughout the Womble world. Like all good cooks she stands no nonsense in her kitchen and has been known to rap even Tobermory's paws when he tried to taste one of her bracken jellies before it was properly set.

The Wombles keep well clear of people, as they feel that if grown-up humans started getting inquisitive about the way the Wombles work the Wombles wouldn't get a moment's peace. However, they quite like human children and talk to them from time to time, for the Wombles are great talkers, and just about the worst punishment that Great Uncle Bulgaria can give anyone is to 'send them to Coventry'.

There are Womble communities everywhere, for as Great Uncle Bulgaria so rightly says, 'If it wasn't for us Wombles clearing up behind them, Human Beings would be knee-deep in rubbish by now. Silly sort of creatures, Human Beings. I'll NEVER understand them. Not if I live to be THREE hundred! Ho hum!'

CHAPTER ONE

# *The Purple Paw Mystery*

On dark and stormy winter evenings, when the wind is howling through the trees and blowing the rain in all directions at once, the Wombles bolt the doors of their burrow and settle down for a nice, cosy, sociable time.

'I'll never understand Human Beings,' said Bungo, 'I mean – fancy living in a house on a night like this. I bet all the windows rattle and the doors creak . . .'

'And the wind goes "wooooooo" round the chimney pots,' agreed Orinoco, in such a frightening voice that both young Wombles took a quick glance round to make sure that they really *were* safely inside their own warm, friendly burrow.

'What are *you* going to do this evening?' asked Bungo in a rather off-hand way, which showed that he'd got something on his mind.

'I had thought of – well nothing, exactly, quite, that is you know,' replied Orinoco, shifting about on his back paws and avoiding his friend's eyes. There was a moment's awkward silence which was broken by Tomsk, the largest and most athletic of the Wombles, bustling down the passage.

'Hallo,' he said, 'can't stop now. Might be late. 'Bye.'

'Where are you going?' asked Bungo.

'The Recreation Room. Great Uncle Bulgaria's going to tell a story you know.'

'Story Time's for very *young* Wombles,' said Bungo, 'not for working Wombles like us.'

'Is it?' Tomsk said over his shoulder, 'well I don't care. I *like* stories. I'm going to ask for "The Purple Paw Mystery", because I'm in it.'

'So am I,' interrupted Bungo. 'I'm just about the most important Womble in that story and . . .'

'No you're not, I am, if you don't mind my mentioning it,' Tomsk said (he was always very polite), 'and we're going to have hot conkers all nice and sizzling and . . . I say, steady on Orinoco, you nearly pushed me over.'

'Sorry,' mumbled Orinoco and hurried off, calling over his shoulder, 'hot conkers, all sizzling, *de*-licious! Well are you coming or aren't you, Bungo?'

'Well I might, if you insist . . .'

Bungo spoke to the empty air, for the other two had already disappeared into the Recreation Room, so Bungo gave a long-suffering sigh – just in case any other Wombles might be listening, which they weren't – and then trotted after his friends. He'd meant to go to the Story Telling all along, only his dignity wouldn't let him come out into the open and say so. He had been a working Womble for quite a short time, so he had a lot of dignity to worry about.

'Hurry up young Womble,' said Great Uncle Bulgaria, who was sitting in his rocking-chair with rows and rows of young Wombles grouped round him, their little black eyes gleaming with excitement. 'Oh, it's you Bungo. Late as usual! Now sit down and keep quiet. Orinoco, don't stuff too many hot conkers into your mouth at once.'

'MMMMM,' said Orinoco, whose cheeks were bulging.

'Now then,' said Great Uncle Bulgaria, 'on a wild, wet evening like this I think the best story is

"The Purple Paw Mystery". It was a most *mysterious* business . . .' His voice sank lower, and a delighted, shivery feeling ran through the fur of all the listening Wombles. 'This is how this particular story begins . . .'

Great Uncle Bulgaria was sitting in his study writing up the Womble Diary when his pen started to run out of ink. He shook it a few times and the pen worked for a line or two, and then the words got fainter and fainter until they vanished. Great Uncle Bulgaria, usually the most patient of Wombles, was rather annoyed, as he felt he had been writing particularly well. However, he knew that Tobermory was at this very moment making some new ink in the Workshop, so the old Womble pinged the little bell on his desk. Now this ping-ping-ping noise was supposed to be a signal to Tomsk, who was on duty at the main door of the burrow. The instant he heard that ping-ping-ping Tomsk should have gone trotting along to the study to find out what Great Uncle Bulgaria wanted.

Unfortunately Tomsk just happened to be doing some exercises. They were 'running on the spot' followed by 'touch the back paws' and then 'press-ups'. Violent exercises of this kind make even an extremely fit Womble like Tomsk get a kind of singing noise in the head, so that when he finally realized that the ping-ping-ping was not just his muscles making a noise, he decided that he must have heard the inter-burrow-telephone.

'Yes, yes, yes, it's me,' said Tomsk down the

telephone. Naturally enough there was no answer which was rather puzzling.

Great Uncle Bulgaria, who had got tired of shaking his pen and banging on the bell, came out of his study and shouted.

'TOMSK!'

Tomsk did a complete backwards somersault, and came face to face with Great Uncle Bulgaria.

'You great gormless Womble,' said Great Uncle Bulgaria (quite crossly for him, as in the ordinary way he was extremely patient), 'I've been ringing and ringing for you. Now off you go to the Workshop and get some more ink from Tobermory and FILL UP THIS PEN. Shuffle your paws do . . .'

Tomsk did more than that. He sprinted.

In the Workshop Tobermory was very busy hammering away at something or other. Tobermory is always busy. So when Tomsk explained about the need for more ink Tobermory said:

'Over there, young Womble, in that bucket. I've got a lot of the felt bits out of felt-tip pens in there. They need a bit more squeezing and a drop more water and then we'll have some fresh ink. Give it another stir and don't come bothering me about it. I've got plenty on *my* paws as it is . . .'

Tomsk had a look at the bucket and gave it a stir with a hammer. It looked like a very pale sort of ink to him. Not at all the kind of ink that Great Uncle Bulgaria would like, really. And while he was thinking about this he heard the faint ping-ping-ping of that bell again.

'Oh dear,' Tomsk said, 'Tobermory . . .?' but Tobermory was hurrying out of the Workroom with a sheet of hardboard under one arm, a spanner behind his ear and a whole lot of screws in his mouth. The door shut behind him.

'Oh dear,' said Tomsk, 'oh dear, oh dear . . .'

He gave the melting felt tips another stir, but the ink still remained a light violet shade, so Tomsk decided that he'd better do something pretty drastic. He thought about it for several seconds and then, muttering, 'Oh well, here goes . . .',

he put first one back paw into the bucket (there was a delicious squelchy sound) and then his other back paw. And once he'd gone as far as that it was really quite easy to start doing his 'running on the spot' exercises and the deep-bluey-violet colour came squelching out of the old felt tips in a most satisfying way.

Tomsk could have gone on with this interesting new game for some time, but the ping-ping-ping of Great Uncle Bulgaria's bell somehow seemed to be growing louder every second so, now that he had at least half a bucket full of blue-violet-to-black ink, Tomsk climbed out – shaking his back paws vigorously – and then he carefully refilled the pen and took it along to Great Uncle Bulgaria.

'Ho hum,' said Great Uncle Bulgaria, 'you took your time, young Womble. Thank you very much. Back to you duties at the Main Door. Bungo (silly sort of name, but it suits him) and Orinoco (if he's still awake) should be home from tidying-up work any minute now and you'll have to tick their names off in the Duty Book.'

Great Uncle Bulgaria, as usual, was quite right. Tomsk only had a couple of minutes in which to do a few more exercises before Bungo and Orinoco, their tidy-bags absolutely crammed with

23

so-called rubbish which had been left behind by Human Beings, came trudging back towards the burrow.

'One-two-one-two . . .' puffed Tomsk, and with his chin well up and his elbows in to his sides he came dancing out of the burrow to meet them. 'I say you *have* been working hard. So have I actually. I've been . . .'

'Hooray, supper!' said Orinoco, sniffing happily, 'I can smell toadstool and moss pie followed by elmbark mix on fried grass bread. Or it could be . . .'

'Working *hard*?' said Bungo, 'I should say we *have* been working hard. I've picked up fifty-four bus tickets, two copies of *The Times*, sixteen soft-drink tins, five milk cartons, two walking-sticks, one camera, three gloves – all odd ones – a hat and . . . I SAY . . . LOOK AT THAT.'

Bungo's voice changed in such an odd way that Tomsk forgot his own news and Orinoco even stopped trying to work out what they were going to have for supper. Which just goes to show how much Bungo's voice had changed.

All three young Wombles paused and a shiver went right through their fur, for there, right out-side their burrow, were some most peculiar

paw marks. ENORMOUS, SINISTER,
PURPLE PAW-MARKS...

And at the very same moment Great Uncle
Bulgaria drew a neat line at the bottom of the
Womble Diary and put his pen away, and then
he just happened to glance at the floor. From
the door and right up to his desk there
were HORRIBLE, EXTRAORDINARY
PURPLE PAW-MARKS...

Great Uncle Bulgaria felt a shiver run right up and down his back and his white fur went all prickly, because never before in his very long life had he seen paw-marks like these. With great courage he got up, took hold of his stick and began to follow the track of these dreadful paw-marks. What hideous 'SOMETHING' might be waiting outside in the passage to POUNCE on him...

(At this point in the story every Womble in the Recreation Room made a grab for his or her nearest neighbour, while their little button eyes went from left to right and a delicious shudder ran up and down their backs, as they imagined the deep black night and the howling wind outside their cosy burrow. As for Bungo, that working Womble of the World, he was practically underneath Orinoco's chair . . . )

Great Uncle Bulgaria walked quietly and calmly out of his study. Tobermory had come out of his own particular workshop, because somehow he too had sensed that something was not quite right. He fell into step with Great Uncle Bulgaria, and together these two very wise and fearless old Wombles tracked the dreadful purple paw-marks down the passage, up to the main door and then out into the open. They were concentrating so

hard that they didn't even notice Bungo and
Orinoco and Tomsk who were also tracking the
paw-marks, until the five of them met face to face.
It was quite a shock for all of them.

'Wait,' said Great Uncle Bulgaria, raising his
walking-stick. 'I believe we are all on the same
trail.'

'What is it?' whispered Bungo.

'I don't know, but it's right behind *me*,' shivered Orinoco.

'There are three sets of purple paw-marks now,' said Tomsk. 'Look . . .'

They all looked. It was quite true, there was a sort of muddled track of extra purple paw-marks right behind Tomsk.

At this point in the story there was a very long pause, during which all the Wombles looked at Tomsk, who was studying his paws in an off-hand way.

'Whatever IT is, it's after you, Tomsk,' whispered Bungo, while Orinoco's teeth were chattering so hard that they made a noise like Madame Cholet chopping up apple-cores.

'Eeeeee,' said Tomsk, and he would have fallen flat on his face with fright, if Great Uncle Bulgaria hadn't propped him up with his walking-stick.

'Ho ho ho HUM!' said Great Uncle Bulgaria and his wise old eyes began to twinkle. 'I do believe I know what Awful, Dreadful, Terrible thing it is that has been following us round and has even trailed us right into the burrow. Tomsk, young Womble, would you be so kind as to let me have a look at your back paws? One at a time! One at a time or you really will fall flat on your face.'

Tomsk, his eyes tightly closed, did as he was asked.

'Well!' said Tobermory, inspecting first one paw and then the other, 'Tck, tck, tck! Oh dearie me. Tut, tut. Yes, Bulgaria old friend, you've solved our mystery for us and it's just about the worst case of purple-paw-itis I've ever seen. In fact it's the *only* one I've ever seen.'

'What . . . what . . . what do you mean?' asked Tomsk, slowly opening one eye and squinting over his shoulder at the solemn-faced Tobermory.

'It means you great . . .' said Great Uncle

Bulgaria, prodding the tottering Tomsk with his stick, 'gormless', prod, 'Womble', prod-prod, 'That it's YOUR paw-marks we've all been following. Perhaps you would be good enough to explain why you decided to try and dye your paws purple. IF it's not too much to ask.'

Tomsk did his best, but it took some while, what with having to describe the business of the pinging bell and the press-ups; but he got it all straight in the end, by which time poor Orinoco's stomach was rumbling quite loudly for its supper.

'I see,' said Great Uncle Bulgaria, 'Of course, Tobermory and I never believed for one moment that any purple-pawed monster had actually entered our burrow. *I* should never allow it to happen for a start! Well, well what are we all hanging about here for? There's toadstool and moss pie for supper with elmbark mix on fried grass bread for afters. Tomsk, please clean your paws thoroughly before entering. A purple-pawed monster indeed. Tck, tck, tck . . .'

At this point in the story Great Uncle Bulgaria stopped speaking and every head in the Recreation Room turned to look at Tomsk who shuffled and squirmed about in his chair.

'But,' continued Great Uncle Bulgaria, when the silence had gone on just long enough, 'we have learnt two most important things from this story. The first is that we Wombles are perfectly safe in this burrow and the second is that thanks to Tomsk there's a most efficient paw method of producing ink. Now then, off to bed with the lot of you. That's the end of Story Time for tonight . . .'

'I tell you what,' said Orinoco, somewhat indistinctly as his cheeks were full of the last of the hot (quite delicious) conkers, 'that's just about my favourite story. I mean I'm about the most important Womble in it really. If it hadn't been for me . . .'

'You?' said Bungo, 'it was *me* that was important. If it hadn't been for me seeing . . .'

'No it wasn't,' said Tomsk. 'I was the Womble who . . .'

All three young Wombles now began to punch each other in a friendly way as the argument continued out into the passage. Great Uncle Bulgaria watched them go while he leant on his stick and shook his white head.

'Tck, tck, tck,' he murmured, 'all of 'em working Wombles and yet they still enjoy Story Time, and quite right too. Of course what none of them realizes is that I take the leading role in the Purple Paw Mystery. Why, if it hadn't been for me ... why, hallo Tobermory, old friend. It's a wild night outside. Very wild. Why Human Beings choose to live in houses and flats instead of nice and snugly underground I'll never understand.'

'Nor me,' said Tobermory, 'not if I live to be TWO hundred. But with a high wind like this there'll be a lot of so-called rubbish for us Wombles to clear up tomorrow.'

'Then we'll *worry* about it tomorrow,' said Great Uncle Bulgaria, 'come along to my study and we'll have a nice hot cup of elmbark broth. Story-telling is a very exhausting business, old friend ...'

# CHAPTER TWO

# Peep-peep-peep

There had been such a strong wind during the night that a great deal of rubbish had been blown in all directions. Of all the kinds of weather this is the sort that the Wombles most dislike as it means they have to work harder than ever, hence the old saying, 'A high wind at night is no Womble's delight.'

Great Uncle Bulgaria murmured this under his breath as he stood at the main door of the burrow and looked about him. There was a great deal to look at, too, as there were newspapers, plastic bottles, bus tickets, sweet wrappers, paper-bags, tins, packets, comics and bits of this and pieces of that in all directions.

'Human Beings,' said Great Uncle Bulgaria, 'are without doubt the most untidy, wasteful,

33

irresponsible creatures in the whole world. If it wasn't for us Wombles they would have vanished long ago, submerged by their own rubbish. Isn't that right, young Womble?'

'Yes,' agreed Orinoco who was just going on tidying-up duty. Only it sounded more like 'Ye-aaaaah', because – as usual – Orinoco was half asleep on his back paws.

'Stand up straight, do!' ordered Great Uncle Bulgaria sternly.

Orinoco did his best, but it wasn't easy, owing to the roundness of his figure. However, at the most unwelcome sight before him his little black eyes stopped being sleepy and grew wider and wider until they looked like coat buttons.

'Oh lor, oh dear, oh my,' said Orinoco, '*what* a lot of work!'

'Plenty to do, is there?' asked Bungo, bustling up with his tidy-bag over his arm. 'Good.'

Wellington, who was the last of the Wombles on clearing-up duty that particular morning, didn't say anything at all. He just took off his large spectacles and polished them on his scarf and then put them on again, as though he hoped this would make some of the rubbish vanish. It didn't – it just made a lot of it more visible as he could see further. If possible he now looked even sadder than he usually did.

'Working Wombles,' said Great Uncle Bulgaria, 'there is a great deal for you to do today, a very great deal and you will have to cover a lot of ground. Please remember to be careful not to let any Human Beings see you at work. Human Beings are funny sort of creatures and they might start on a great Womble Hunt if they spotted one of us. Small Humans are all right, of course, but none of them will be about at this early hour. Now off you go – and remember – keep in touch with one another. We don't want any Womble to go wandering off so that he gets lost.'

And Great Uncle Bulgaria looked over his spectacles at Wellington, who was rather a dreamy sort of Womble and who had no sense of direction.

'Sorry,' said Wellington. He was always saying it.

'There's nothing to be sorry about – yet,' said Great Uncle Bulgaria. 'Just keep in touch.'

'How are we supposed to keep in touch though?' asked Wellington as Great Uncle Bulgaria, in his stately way, retired into the burrow.

'By waving or whistling or something. *I* don't know,' replied Bungo. 'All I jolly well do know is

that there's an awful lot of rubbish to be tidied up.
Come on . . .'

Bungo and Wellington, moving further and
further apart, started to pick up all the old newspapers and comics and cartons which they stuffed
into their tidy-bags. In fact they worked so hard
that they neither of them noticed that Orinoco
had tiptoed over to a bush and decided to have
about twenty winks in order to get up his strength.

'Hallo,' muttered Wellington, picking up an empty tin can, 'this tin's got a hole in the bottom. Some silly old Human Being must have used an opener on it at the wrong end. And hallo, here's a nice piece of string. Now if I put the end of this piece of string through the hole in the tin and make a knot it'll be an easy way of dragging this old tin behind me, and if I find any more old tins with holes in the bottom of 'em I can join 'em on and hallo, I've found one . . . '

Wellington often talked to himself when he was alone, because he was rather shy and, although the other Wombles in the burrow were all his friends, they didn't often listen to what he was saying.

'Hallo,' Bungo was saying to himself at this particular moment, 'a piece of string. I wonder how long it is? Come on string . . .'

And Bungo gave the piece of string a pull. Now Bungo happened to be at the other end of Wellington's piece of string and at the exact moment that he gave it a tug, so did Wellington. The result was that Bungo's piece of string was pulled out of his paws and went wriggling away across the ground.

'Oi, hey, I say,' said Bungo, 'come back. You

must be a very long wriggly worm sort of string
and oi . . .' and Bungo made a flying leap and
caught hold of the string just before it vanished
into the bushes. Of course, being a Womble, once
he had got hold of something, he couldn't let go
and, although the string now pulled him through
all kinds of rubbish and through bushes, Bungo
still clung on to it. He was flat on his stomach and
his tidy-bag was bumping along behind him.

Poor old Wellington was having a terrible time
too, as he hauled away at the string. But naturally

enough he couldn't let go either, and so in a very short time two astonished young Wombles came face to face.

'I thought it was a wriggly worm,' puffed Bungo.

'A very *heavy* worm,' replied Wellington who was even more out of breath. 'I say Bungo, old chap, I've had an Idea. Would you like to take part in an experiment?'

'Not particularly. What *sort* of experiment?'

'Hang on a tick while I put your end of the string through this tin and knot it like this and then you take that tin over there,' and Wellington waved one paw, 'and put it up against your ear.'

'Will it blow up?' asked Bungo.

'I don't think so. No *of course* not. Go on Bungo,' said Wellington, and for once in his life he didn't apologize because he was so full of his wonderful idea. And for once in *his* life Bungo didn't argue any more, but did as he was told.

The two young Wombles moved further and further apart until the string was quite taut between them, and then Wellington took a deep breath and put his mouth up against his tin and said,

'Peep-peep-peep, this is Wellington calling

Bungo. Do you read me? Put the tin against your mouth to answer. Over.'

Bungo nearly fell flat on his back with surprise. Although Wellington was now quite out of sight he could hear Wellington's voice in his ear. Bungo managed to pull himself together and he put the tin against his own mouth and said rather feebly,

'H-h-hallo. I mean Peep-peep-peep. It's me you know, Bungo. C-c-calling Wellington. I say its rather fun, isn't it? How does it work? Over.'

'I don't exactly know. Not quite exactly,' buzzed Wellington's voice in Bungo's ear. 'So you'd better come back. Over and out.'

Bungo, his eyes shining, trotted across to his friend and hit him affectionately on the back.

'I say Wellington,' he said, 'you *are* clever. You've invented the first "keep-in-touch" Womble telephone. Well done. How did you do it?'

'Ah,' said Wellington who was very unsure

about this himself, 'well, ho hum. That is. I tell
you what, let's see if it works on Orinoco too.
He's dozing away under that bush there . . .'

Very carefully and on tiptoe the two
young Wombles put one tin very firmly up against
Orinoco's ear.

'Zzzzzzzz,' said Orinoco, scratching himself
sleepily, 'dandelion pie . . . zzzzzzz . . .'

'Now move backwards,' whispered Wellington,
retreating step by step with Bungo at his side.
'right back to the door of the burrow should do
it . . . hallo . . . oh!'

'Ho hum,' said Great Uncle Bulgaria, who had
been standing in the doorway for the last ten
minutes, thoroughly enjoying what was going on.
'Dear me, you have been working hard! Why,
your tidy-bags are quite full! Well done!'

'Yes, but . . .' said Bungo.

'But, yes, sorry, I mean . . .' said Wellington.

'There's no need to keep on apologizing,' said

Great Uncle Bulgaria, picking up the tin and looking at it and then sniffing at it and putting it to his ear. 'Dear me! Ho hum! I seem to hear a distant zzzzzzzz noise. How very odd! How very strange! How most mysterious.'

And Great Uncle Bulgaria's wise old eyes looked at the two young Wombles and started to twinkle. He put a white paw on Wellington's shoulder and said softly.

'Why I do believe you may have invented the very first ever Womble keep-in-touch telephone, Wellington. And I daresay it will turn out to be a most useful invention at that. One that deserves a double helping of dandelion pie with raspberry cream topping. Off you go. You too Bungo.'

'But,' said Wellington, 'I'm sorry but I don't know exactly how this invention works, you know.'

'Don't let it worry you,' said Great Uncle Bulgaria. 'As long as it *does* work, that's the important part. Now away you go . . .'

Great Uncle Bulgaria waited until the two young Wombles had vanished into the burrow and then he put his mouth right up against the tin and said loudly.

'Peep-peep-peep. This is Great Uncle Bulgaria

calling Orinoco. And how much tidying-up have you done this morning, young Womble? Over!'

The effect on Orinoco was amazing. One moment there he was happily dozing away and the next he was on his trembling back paws trying to make out where this extraordinary voice had come from. He looked all over the place – round the bush, over the bush and under the bush – but there was nobody there. And then a very strange thing happened, because a perfectly ordinary old tin can that was lying in the grass began to

wriggle away from him. Orinoco's fur rose up into prickles as he watched it.

'Peep-peep-peep' said a familiar voice apparently out of the thin air. 'This is Great Uncle Bulgaria. The time now is fifteen seconds after dinner-time and it's dandelion pie with raspberry cream. But young Wombles who don't do any work don't get any pie. Over and out . . .'

And with these dreadful words the old tin can was jerked out of sight through the bushes and vanished. Orinoco started after it and once again his little black eyes grew round as coat buttons.

''straordinary . . .' muttered Orinoco, beginning to clear up all the surrounding rubbish as fast as he could go, ''straordinary. I'm sure I heard Great Uncle Bulgaria's voice and that there was a tin that wriggled away like a worm. I must have imagined it. I must have dreamed it all. And a very nasty dream it was too. Perhaps I should have kept in touch with all the other working Wombles just like Great Uncle Bulgaria ordered . . . Oh dear, oh lor, oh me! . . .'

Orinoco paused in his frantic work and rubbed a front paw across his forehead as he added,

'I do *hope* they manage to keep some dandelion pie – with raspberry cream topping – for me . . .'

(They did.)

# CHAPTER THREE

# *The Invisible Womble*

Orinoco was very worried about himself and for once in his life it wasn't his stomach that he was fretting about. It was all of him.

'I don't feel at all fit,' he said, shaking his head and giving his tubby little body a good scratch. Of all the Wombles, none of whom are exactly what you'd call thin, he was by far the fattest, which means he was very plump indeed.

'I say Bungo, old chap,' said Orinoco as Bungo hurried past him in the burrow, 'I don't feel at all fit, you know.'

'You look all right to me,' said Bungo, 'a bit

overweight perhaps, but that's all. Now, if you don't mind, I'm in rather a hurry.'

'You always are,' muttered Orinoco, and he was quite right as Bungo was inclined to be busy and bossy most of the time.

Orinoco heaved a deep sigh and went to see Tomsk who was doing skipping exercises in the Recreation Room.

'I say Tomsk, old chap,' said Orinoco, 'I don't feel at all fit you know. In fact I feel quite poorly.'

'What you need,' said Tomsk, skipping away, like anything, 'is more exercise, twenty-one, twenty-two, twenty-three.'

'No I don't,' said Orinoco crossly.

'Twenty-four, twenty-five, twenty-six. There's another skipping-rope over there, come and join me. Twenty-seven twenty-eight, twenty-nine.'

'Hah,' said Orinoco bitterly and he stumped off to the kitchen where Madame Cholet was in the middle of preparing one of her extra-specially-delicious stews. The smell was so lovely that for a few moments it quite put all Orinoco's troubles out of his mind.

'Well?' demanded Madame Cholet, reaching up for another shining saucepan which was hooked onto the springmattress that was bolted to the

ceiling of the kitchen. (The transformation of the mattress into a saucepan and frying-pan holder had been one of Tobermory's very best ideas.)

'No, not at *all* well,' replied Orinoco. 'In fact, far from it.'

'*Tiens*!' said Madame Cholet who spoke French from time to time as she had a French name. 'You look perfectly fit to me. Perhaps a little less food and more work would do you good. Kindly pass me that knife, also the wooden spoon and take your greedy paws off those holly-berries, as I need them for my casserole. Also, now that you are here, you can assist me with the washing-up and with chopping those leaves and . . . *tiens*! He has vanished! Tck, tck, tck . . .'

And Madame Cholet shook her head, chuckled and then returned to her cooking.

'Nobody understands, nobody sympathizes,' Orinoco said to himself as he plodded off down the passage, his head down and his paws clasped behind his back. He was completely unaware that Great Uncle Bulgaria was standing in his study doorway, watching him. 'Nobody cares, nobody – I say watch out!'

'Sorry,' said Wellington, who had just come out of the Library with his nose, as usual, buried in a

book. 'Did I bash into you? Sorry. I say Orinoco, I'm reading an awfully interesting book. It's all about camouflage and . . .'

'Never heard of him,' said Orinoco grumpily.

'It's not a him, it's an it. It's . . .'

'One of those humpy animals that live in deserts, I know . . .'

'No you don't,' contradicted Wellington in his serious way as he marked his place in the book with a silver-paper book-mark, 'that's a camel. Although I suppose you could camouflage a camel and then you'd have a camel-flage.'

Wellington looked over the top of his round spectacles with a hopeful expression, but Orinoco's sulky face didn't change.

'It was a joke,' said Wellington, 'You see – oh well, never mind. Anyway, if you camouflage something it vanishes – sort of. It's there all the time really, but you can't really *see* it so you think it's disappeared and . . .'

'Which is what'll happen to me,' interrupted Orinoco, who felt that Wellington had been talking far too much. 'I shall vanish quite away and everyone will be dreadfully sorry that they didn't listen to me.'

'I say,' said Wellington, his eyes gleaming, 'how

*clever*! How will you do it, Orinoco? Can I watch?'

Orinoco opened and shut his mouth a couple of times, while Wellington stared at him, holding his breath in case Orinoco chose that exact moment to do his vanishing trick. But Orinoco remained as solid as ever (which was very solid indeed) and then, quite rudely for a Womble, he snapped.

'For such a clever sort of Womble you can be very silly. I mean I shall get thinner and thinner and THINNER until there's nothing of me left.'

'Will you?' Wellington said doubtfully.

'Yes. I will. So there. I've been overworking, but nobody cares. Nobody's interested. What I need is a good forty winks, or perhaps eighty winks to get my strength up again, but shall I get them? No . . .' Orinoco said hurriedly, just in case Wellington answered him, 'and why not?' He was speaking in a gabble now, 'because I'm on tidying-up work, that's why not and working is very, very bad for a Womble in my state of health. It may even be disastrous. So there!'

And off went Orinoco feeling thoroughly badly-done-by and thoroughly out-of-sorts and alto-gether cross and itching.

'I *am* sorry,' said Wellington, 'I wish I could help . . .'

As Wellington was extremely kind-hearted he worried quite a lot about Orinoco, and when he went off with Bungo on tidying-up work he tried to explain why he was so worried.

'Orinoco – vanish!' said Bungo, 'never!'

'But he's not well, you know,' said Wellington, shaking his head so sadly that his large round spectacles slid right down his nose.

'There's only one thing wrong with him,' replied Bungo, 'underworking and over-eating. I say, there's a piece of rope under that bush. Tomsk'll like that. He'll be able to make himself another skipping-rope. He keeps wearing them out. Lend us a paw, young Wellington.'

'Are you sure?' asked Wellington.

'Course I'm sure. I know a piece of old rope when I see it.'

'No, sorry, I mean about Orinoco not being really ill.'

'Yes,' said Bungo, who was always sure about everything. 'Come on . . .'

'Sorry,' said Wellington, 'well it is a relief to hear you say that. Oh, Bungo – it's not just a piece of rope after all. It's a fishing net.'

'No it isn't. It's – it's a – a – um – it's a tennis net.'

'Oh?'

'It's a net curtain thing that Human Beings play tennis over. Don't you know anything, young Womble?'

'Not much, no,' agreed Wellington, 'except that the correct height for a tennis net is 3 foot 6 inches at the posts and that the net-court judge in a tennis championship has to keep his finger lightly on the top of the net during service. This is because – shall I go on, Bungo?'

Bungo, his front paws full of old tennis net, paused, looked at Wellington's innocent face and then shook his head. There were times when even Bungo realized that other Wombles might know more about certain subjects than he did. Not often, but sometimes. It was rather lowering to his dignity, so he was quite glad to see Orinoco, an empty tidy-bag loosely clasped in one paw, coming slowly towards them.

'What I need,' said Orinoco to nobody in particular, 'is a nice forty to eighty winks to get my strength back. Too much work and no rest, stops a Womble from feeling his best. There's a lot of truth in these old proverbs.'

'What you need . . . um, um um,' said Bungo as Wellington suddenly put a paw over his mouth.

'What you really need,' said Wellington, 'is to become invisible. I think you should become the first invisible Womble.'

'Oh? Do you?' said Orinoco suspiciously. 'Why?'

'Because – because then you could have a little nap and nobody else would know about it,' replied Wellington who suddenly realized that he had been spending a lot of good reading time worrying about a friend who wasn't ill at all, but only suffering from a fit of the sulks and too much over-eating.

'It *sounds* quite a good idea,' said Orinoco cautiously.

'Mmmmmmmm,' said Bungo, who still had a paw over his mouth.

'It *is* a good idea,' replied Wellington, 'I'll camelflage – sorry – camouflage you and then no-body'll be able to see if you're really there or not.'

'Ho hum,' said Great Uncle Bulgaria who was standing quietly at the door of the burrow listening to all this.

'How will you do it?' asked Orinoco, who was still just a bit suspicious of the whole idea.

'With an old tennis – sorry – camouflage net,' replied Wellington. 'Bungo and I will just push a few leaves into some of the holes and then we'll put the net over you and you'll be invisible.'

'Really? That's astonishing,' said Orinoco.

'Yes, *isn't* it! Come on Bungo,' said Wellington, who'd had to take his paw away from Bungo's mouth in order to hold it over his own to stop himself from laughing.

Orinoco, quite overcome by this sudden change in his luck, stood like a statue while Bungo and Wellingon carefully threw the net over his tubby shape and then, even more carefully, helped him totter to the nearest bush, where he lay down.

'I shay,' said Orinoco somewhat thickly through both the net and the leaves, which were tickling his nose, 'I shay, am I really invisible?'

'Rather,' said Bungo as Wellington nudged him. 'Um, yes . . .'

''shtraordinary,' muttered Orinoco, 'I'll jusht have forty winks then . . .'

'Quite "shtraordinary",' agreed Wellington, who was wheezing almost as much as Orinoco because he was trying not to laugh.

'Psst,' said Bungo behind his paw to Wellington, 'I don't understand why we've made him invisible.'

'You'll see,' said Wellington, and added, 'heh heh heh . . .'

Bungo and Wellington worked very hard for the next hour, picking up all kinds of rubbish. Bungo had a thoughtful frown on his face, but Wellington just kept smiling, although from time to time he had to put down his tidy-bag so that he could go 'heh heh heh' in comfort.

Orinoco just snored.

Great Uncle Bulgaria, a slight smile on his old face, tiptoed back into the burrow. Once there he drew out his enormous pocket handkerchief, blew his nose and then went, 'heh heh heh. Too

57

much work and no rest stops a Womble from feeling his best, indeed. Too much food and no work makes a fat Womble shirk! would be nearer the mark. Heh heh heh. Now I wonder what's for supper? What partic-ular-ly delicious meal is Madame Cholet cooking for us? Ho hum.'

The tidy-bags of Bungo and Wellington were full to the brim by the time the supper-bell rang. It acted like magic on the pair of them.

'Supper,' said Wellingon, his nose quivering.

'About time too,' said Bungo.

'Shupper,' said Orinoco, stirring in his sleep.

'Supper-time for all working Wombles,' said Great Uncle Bulgaria, appearing in the doorway of the burrow and leaning on his stick. 'And tonight it's Madame Cholet's extra-specially-delicious casserole with fried brambles and dandelions, a touch of moss-garlic, sliced oak apples, a pinch of elmbark and a bubbling crust of toadstools all golden brown. Dear me,' and the old Womble, quite carried away by his own words, had to pause and take a deep breath.

'Casserole,' breathed Bungo.

'Fried brambles,' murmured Wellington, his spectacles misting over at this lovely thought.

'Slished oak appleshes,' grunted Orinoco who

was quite suddenly wide-awake and feeling very fit indeed. He tried to get up, but his paws were so entangled in the netting that all he could manage to do was to roll over, which made him more tangled up than ever.

'Help,' said Orinoco, 'I shay Bungo, Wellington, help . . .'

'Tell me,' said Wellington, putting one paw to his ear and looking up at the evening sky, 'did you hear something then, Bungo?'

'Yes, I heard Orino-ouch,' said Bungo.

'An invisible Womble,' said Wellington, taking his back paw off Bungo's back paw and continuing to look dreamily up at the darkening clouds, 'an INVISIBLE Womble would have an INVISIBLE voice, wouldn't you think?'

Bungo rubbed his paw, then he looked at Wellington and then at their two full tidy-bags and then at Orinoco's empty tidy-bag; and finally he looked at a rolled-up ball of netting which was swaying backwards and forwards.

'Ah,' said Bungo thoughtfully, 'yes, yes I think you're probably quite correct about that Wellington, old friend. And what's more an INVISIBLE Womble would have an INVISIBLE stomach I daresay.'

Orinoco stopped rolling about as he heard these words and his little black eyes grew round, as buttons.

'Itsh not true,' he said feebly. 'It's my shtomach and I *know* – it's very real indeed . . .'

'Supper-time,' repeated Great Uncle Bulgaria. 'All *working* Wombles need their food to keep up their strength. In you come. Ah Ha! What nice full tidy-bags. You *have* been working hard. Go and wash your paws . . .'

Bungo and Wellington reached the front door of the burrow and then stopped and glanced at each other and shuffled about a bit. A joke is a joke, but nobody likes to carry it too far.

'I say,' said Bungo, 'I say, Great Uncle Bulgaria, about Orinoco . . .'

'Orinoco?' said Great Uncle Bulgaria in a very surprised voice, 'ORINOCO? What about Orinoco? Where *is* Orinoco I wonder. I thought he was supposed to be on tidying-up duty . . .' Great Uncle Bulgaria raised his voice so that it was now quite loud, 'but all I can see of Orinoco is his EMPTY tidy-bag.'

'He's really over there, you know,' said Wellington tugging at Great Uncle Bulgaria's tartan shawl. 'He thinks he's invisible, but he isn't. Not really he isn't . . .'

'Quite,' agreed Great Uncle Bulgaria and winked. Then he put his white paws on the shoulders of the young Wombles and very gently, but extremely firmly, propelled them into the burrow.

'And now,' said Great Uncle Bulgaria to the evening shadows, 'I suppose I must start searching for a certain invisible Womble.'

'I'm here. It's me,' said Orinoco in a very small

voice as the old Womble walked slowly in his direction. 'It is, honeshtly, bother these leaves, it's me.'

'Orinoco,' mused Great Uncle Bulgaria, leaning on his stick and admiring the brightness of the evening star, 'a promising young Womble in many ways, but far too fond of his stomach. If he ate less and worked more he would certainly feel fitter and not so sorry for himself. It's a pity if he *has* become invisible, because we should all miss him a great deal in the burrow . . .'

'Ooooooo,' said a very small voice indeed.

'Good gracious me,' said Great Uncle Bulgaria, almost dropping his stick, he was so startled by this little sound, 'why I do believe I can see a nose and a paw and another paw . . .'

'Yes you can,' agreed Orinoco quickly, 'it's me, I'm here. I'm visible again, aren't I?'

'Why I do believe you are,' said Great Uncle Bulgaria, starting to unwrap the netting. 'And what's more, so is your empty tidy-bag. Now let me see how does that old proverb go? A Womble who lazes his time away . . .'

'Gets no food at the end of the day . . .' finished Orinoco. He heaved a truly tremendous sigh and then shrugged off the last bits of netting. He looked,

for him, quite small and bedraggled in the star-
light as he stood there with his chin on his chest.

'I'll never be invisible again, not ever,' said
Orinoco.

'Good,' said Great Uncle Bulgaria, 'I'm glad to
hear it. Now as soon as that tidy-bag is full you
can come back to the burrow and have your supper. You'd better get a move on, young Womble.'

'Yes, Great Uncle Bulgaria,' said Orinoco, beginning to work at double-quick speed. In fact he worked so fast (and he had got the net to push into his tidy-bag) that he managed to catch up with Great Uncle Bulgaria at the burrow door. (The old Womble had been moving very slowly so that he could admire the full beauty of the night sky.)

'And how do you feel now?' asked Great Uncle Bulgaria.

'Much better,' said Orinoco, 'Quite extraordinarily fit really. I say, Great Uncle Bulgaria, do you think there'll be just a tiny little portion of casserole left for me?'

'Well,' said Great Uncle Bulgaria thoughtfully, 'I shouldn't be at all surprised if your particular friends, Tomsk, Bungo and Wellington, haven't persuaded Madame Cholet to put a nice tasty helping aside for you in the warmer. A sort of *visible* symbol of their friendship for you. Ho hum.'

As usual, of course, Great Uncle Bulgaria was perfectly right.

CHAPTER FOUR

# A Breath of Fresh Air

'Atish-ooooo!' yelled Great Uncle Bulgaria in his study and his papers were blown in all directions by his quite enormous sneeze. 'Tck, tck, tck,' said the old Womble as he blew his nose. 'What's the matter with the burrow at the moment? A Womble can't do anything without . . . without . . .' his voice rose, 'WITHOUT . . . ATIS-HOOOOOOO!!!!!'

This time the sneeze was so violent that little puffs and swirls of dust made the study look quite hazy for a moment or two, and Great Uncle

66

Bulgaria had to take off both his pairs of spectacles to give them a good clean. Then, holding his handkerchief over his nose, he went off to have a word with Tobermory in the Workshop.

A large notice had been pinned on the Workshop door. It said:

'All Wombles are requested to brush themselves down CAREFULLY before entering. Positively no dusty Wombles admitted. Delicate repair work in operation. Signed Tobermory. PS. This means YOU!'

'Tck, tck, tck,' said Great Uncle Bulgaria, only – because he was speaking through his handkerchief – it came out sounding like 'Tssshh, tssshhh, tssshhh.' 'Well, well, one must abide by the rules . . .'

Great Uncle Bulgaria took off his tartan shawl and gave it a good shake, and then he patted his white fur (he was so old his fur was the colour of new snow) and finally he took off his little tartan cap and gave it a couple of sharp taps with his paw. Quite a bit of dust went drifting off down the burrow and Great Uncle Bulgaria had to put his paw quickly under his nose to stop himself from sneezing as he knocked on the door.

'Come in,' said Tobermory, 'who is it now? Oh,

it's you Bulgaria. Got the sneezing problem have you? So have I! Done my best to fight it, but I haven't found the right answer yet.'

'Goodness gracious me,' said Great Uncle Bulgaria mildly as he looked at his old friend, who was wearing white overalls and a kind of helmet made out of a saucepan lid. But what made Tobermory look really strange was a white handkerchief, two corners of which were knotted round the knob on the top of the lid so that the rest of the handkerchief was draped round his nose.

'Dear, dear me,' said Great Uncle Bulgaria, 'Tobermory, you resemble some dreadful masked bandit.'

'I know I do,' said Tobermory, the handkerchief blowing in and out with every word, 'but how can I possibly put the bits of three old clocks together in order to make one good, reliable clock, if I keep sneezing every other second? This is my own anti-dust kit, but it's not at all satisfactory The handkerchief tickles my nose and that makes me want to start sneezing again. The burrow's absolutely full of dust and it is most inconvenient and . . .'

Tobermory went on for quite a while in a

grumbling sort of way, and Great Uncle Bulgaria nodded and made comforting sounds of agreement, and at the finish Tobermory's usual calm good humour was quite restored. He undid the handkerchief mask and used it to blow his nose and then shook his grey head.

'Sorry,' he said gruffly, 'but I get very tired of fiddly little watch-springs and screws and bits of this and that blowing in all directions because of my sneezing. It's the weather that's done it. This long, dry spell of hot sunshine has made even the grass turn grey with dust, and so of course every Womble who is on tidying-up duty brings in more dust, and so the problem gets worse and worse. What's the answer Bulgaria?'

'A nice clean, cool, refreshing shower of rain, old friend. But until that happens I'm afraid we shall just have to carry on as best we can. Never mind, perhaps one of our young Wombles will discover some quite different solution to the problem.'

'Perhaps,' agreed Tobermory doubtfully. He glanced at his wrist watch, 'which reminds me, they're due back any moment now from tidying-up duty. Excuse me, Bulgaria,' and Tobermory seized a somewhat bedraggled old carpet brush which had printed round the handle 'Royal Park

Hotel. Not to be taken away.' Somebody or other, however, *had* taken it very far away and furthermore had dumped it on the grass. Tobermory had been meaning to give it new bristles for some weeks but, as he always had at least one-hundred-and-one jobs on hand, he hadn't quite got round to doing it yet.

Tobermory reached the front door of the burrow just as Tomsk, Wellington and Bungo came tramping across the grass with their tidy-bags absolutely stuffed with rubbish. Some yards behind them was Orinoco. *His* tidy-bag held precisely two bus tickets, three elastic bands, a plastic hair slide and two used match-sticks. However, he didn't seem at all worried about having picked up so little. In fact he was smiling right across his round face.

'Tck, tck, tck,' said Tobermory to Orinoco, after he had inspected the other three tidy-bags and muttered, 'well done Tomsk, congratulations Wellington, been busy I see Bungo. But as for *you* Orinoco, *you* don't seem to have done much. Been having a nice forty winks I suppose. Ho hum. Now stand still do. I've got to de-dust you. Oh – oh – O H . . .'

Tobermory made a grab for his handkerchief and just managed to stop himself sneezing.

'I say, yes, but look here,' said Orinoco, 'ouch! ow! ooooo!'

Orinoco stopped trying to speak for a moment as Tobermory began to de-dust him with the old broom so that clouds of dust went flying up into the hot still air.

'Turn round young Womble,' grunted Tobermory and then added in quite a different voice, 'hallo, what have you got behind your back? Goodness gracious me!'

'I did try to tell you,' said Orinoco in a very long-suffering way. 'It was a piece of rubbish I found which was so big I couldn't get it into my tidy-bag. And it was dreadfully heavy to drag along so I'm exhausted and . . .'

'Dear, dear me,' said Tobermory inspecting the rusty, dusty, battered, dented, bedraggled object that Orinoco had been trailing along behind himself. 'I do believe it's what is called a vacuum cleaner. I've heard of them, of course, but I've never actually seen one before. How interesting.'

'What does it do exactly?' asked Bungo.

'Do you play games with it?' rumbled Tomsk. (He was so good at games himself he hardly ever thought of anything else.)

'How does it work?' asked Wellington.

'It sucks up rubbish into this little bag here. No, you don't play games with it. And it works on electricity. How VERY interesting . . .'

And Tobermory hurried back into the burrow, all his crossness quite forgotten, for he really enjoyed playing about with machinery and taking it to pieces and examining it and then putting it back together again. Quite often when Tobermory did this the machinery worked far better and more efficiently than it had ever done before. But then as Great Uncle Bulgaria so rightly said, Tobermory was a real crafts-Womble.

'Here, here, I say! . . .' called Orinoco. 'It was me that found it, you know. And if it does suck up rubbish then it should be me that uses it. Right?'

But Orinoco spoke only to the empty, warm, still summer air. Everybody else had followed Tobermory back into the burrow and into the Workshop in order to get a close-up view of this amazing piece of dumped so-called (by Human Beings) rubbish.

'Drat!' said Orinoco and went after them.

The following ten minutes were extremely interesting as everybody crowded round Tobermory to watch him take the cleaner to pieces. He examined each bit and went 'ho hum. Hum ho', under his breath, 'ah, I see. At least I think I do . . . ah . . . yes, tck, tck, tck. Fancy that! Dear me! Ah!'

'Will it really breathe in rubbish?' asked Orinoco from the back of the group, 'because if it does, I found it you know . . .'

'Shh,' said Great Uncle Bulgaria sternly, 'well

Tobermory old friend, are you ready to demonstrate?'

'I'm not too certain,' replied Tobermory, 'but I'm willing to have a go. Will you all please stand well back just in case . . . I may not have got it put together again quite correctly. There is *one* small point that bothers me . . . however . . . are we all ready? Good. I shall plug it in to my mobile generator.'

'What's that?' whispered Tomsk.

'A car battery on a push-chair,' replied Bungo, 'but mobile generator sounds much more exciting, doesn't it?'

'Shhh!' ordered Great Uncle Bulgaria.

'And I shall now do a count down,' went on Tobermory, who had a slight frown across his face, 'though why I shouldn't count up I am not sure. Ready? Ten, nine, eight, seven, six, five, four, three, two, one, zero – switch on . . . O H!'

What happened during the next ten seconds no Womble who was present at this particular time was ever likely to forget. For Tobermory, who, after all, had never used a vacuum cleaner before, *had* got one small point wrong and instead of sucking air IN the machine blew it OUT. Papers, pots, pans, tools, dust and even Wombles found themselves caught up in a hurricane. Everything and everybody went flying, and a perfect volley of sneezes broke out.

'Atissssshoo.'

'ATTissssshOOOO.'

'AtishssshOOOOOOOOO.'

'Turn it off-shoooo,' ordered Great Uncle Bulgaria from the swirling darkness.

Tobermory did so and slowly, very slowly, everybody, their front paws held under their noses and their eyes watering, got to their back paws. Papers, cardboard, plastic containers and bits of this and that came floating down on top of them.

'Perhaps it doesn't work quite correctly yet, Tobermory old friend,' said Great Uncle Bulgaria, cleaning both his pairs of spectacles on the end of his shawl.

'Not quite right perhaps,' agreed Tobermory, wiping the edge of his apron round his eyes. 'But it will. Wellington, you can help me.'

'Yesh, Tobermory,' said Wellington, who couldn't see anything at all because his spectacles were quite misted over.

For the rest of the night Tobermory and Wellington were extremely busy in

the Workshop. They took this to pieces and that to bits and they made use of three elastic bands, a plastic hair slide and two used match-sticks. And at the finish they looked at each other and Tobermory said gruffly,

'Not bad, young Womble. Thank you very much. Now I want you to volunteer to use the cleaner first thing in the morning. Right?'

'Yes, rather, RIGHT,' said Wellington, 'I SAY!'

'Ho hum,' agreed Tobermory, 'we'll see . . .'

Bungo and then Tomsk and then Wellington came on duty the following still dry and dusty morning. Orinoco trundled along behind them and Great Uncle Bulgaria, leaning on his stick, said to nobody in particular:

'No clouds yet, not a sign of rain. Tck, tck, tck . . .'

Tobermory appeared in the doorway of the burrow holding in front of him part of the cleaner. Only today it looked just a little bit different as part of it was also part of the old broom.

'This,' said Tobermory, 'is the new improved-Tobermory-Wellington vacuum cleaner. It has

been thoroughly tested and we can now guarantee that it will suck up all kinds of rubbish. Will a volunteer please step forwards to . . . oh! '

'Me . . .' said Orinoco just a split second ahead of Wellington who was still half asleep on his back paws. '*I* found it you know. It was *me* that discovered it. So if anybody is going to use it, it should be *me*. That's fair, isn't it? '

There was a slight pause during which Tobermory looked at Great Uncle Bulgaria and then at Wellington and finally at Orinoco. Then Tobermory began to smile and nod, although his voice was very serious as he said,

'Very well, Orinoco. How *good* of you to offer. Well, fellow Wombles, I believe that a way has been found to de-dust the burrow. It is, I think, the perfect answer to our sneeze-problem. Step up Orinoco . . .'

'But I say, I thought it was . . .' said Orinoco rather uneasily. 'I mean, if you'd rather it was somebody else like Wellington who . . .'

'No, go on Orinoco,' said Wellington, his little black eyes twinkling behind his round spectacles. 'That's fair. After all it was you that found the cleaner . . .'

'Yes, but . . . oooooooooo,' said Orinoco.

And no wonder, for Tobermory had just switched on and the very first ever de-dusting-Womble-cleaner had now hummed into action. The brush that Tobermory was holding in his front paws zoomed up and down Orinoco's fur, making it stand on end while it sucked out all the dust, and at the same time it made Orinoco vibrate from top to toe.

'H-h-h-ooooo,' said Orinoco while everybody else watched. 'Ooooooo . . .'

'Very clever,' said Great Uncle Bulgaria.' Most ingenious. Well done. It's the best way of de-dusting both Wombles and the burrow that one can ask for. Congratulations, Tobermory, and you too, Wellington. So now we can all stop sneezing until the Spring showers start. Don't you agree, Orinoco?'

'Oooooooo,' replied Orinoco and then, as Tobermory switched off the machine, he stopped going round and round, shook himself a couple of times and sighed. 'Yes,' said Orinoco sadly, 'I agree.'

He couldn't help feeling just a bit hard-done-by, because he'd been thinking how wonderful it would be to go out on tidying-up duty with a vacuum cleaner. After all, how easy work would become if he could just go whooshing about, sucking in pieces of rubbish, without having to bend and scrabble under bushes with a pointed stick. But now this beautiful dream was over, because his cleaner was only going to be used to de-dust the burrow and the Wombles.

A white paw tapped Orinoco on the shoulder and Great Uncle Bulgaria said quietly.

'Cheer up, young Womble. You've done the burrow a great service. You – and Tobermory

and Wellington – have solved the sneezing problem.'

'Um! Yes,' agreed Orinoco, a little doubtfully.

'And one day the cleaner you tidied up *might*
be used outside the burrow, it's certain to rain
sometime, isn't it? And when that happens we
won't have to worry about dust.'

'Ah,' said Orinoco, thinking this over. His
round face stopped being sad and became its
usual cheerful self. 'Yes, I daresay you're right
Great Uncle Bulgaria. Oh well, I suppose I'd
better start work. Excuse me.'

As Orinoco ambled off across the grass Great

Uncle Bulgaria watched him out of sight, and then a familiar tickling sensation started at the back of his nose and he made a grab for his handkerchief.

'Ah – ah – AH . . .' said Great Uncle Bulgaria, his eyes watering.

'What you need, old friend,' said Tobermory, 'is to be de-dusted. Stand still and I'll switch on.'

'But, but, but . . .' protested Great Uncle Bulgaria. 'Atissssshhhooo . . .'

Tobermory pressed the switch and the first ever de-dusting-Womble-Cleaner hummed efficiently into action once again.

CHAPTER FIVE

# Bungo's Birthday Surprise

Bungo was feeling very unhappy. The reason was that it was his birthday and nobody, none of the other Wombles that is, seemed to have remembered this extremely important fact. He'd got up this morning feeling so excited that he'd been the first in to breakfast. In fact he hurried into the dining-room so early that he was the only one there until Madame Cholet, that marvellous Womble cook, peered through the serving-hatch and said in a distracted voice.

'Who is that? You are too soon. I am not at all ready – oh, it is little Bungo . . .'

'Not so little now. You see I'm older by a whole year because it's my . . .'

'*Un moment*,' said Madame Cholet in French, 'I have so much on my mind. Here is your nettle porridge. Oh, *la la*, it has not set . . .'

'What – the porridge?'

'No, no, no. Not the porridge. The . . .' said Madame Cholet and rattled down the hatch, before Bungo could hear the rest of the sentence.

So he ate his porridge (which as usual was quite

deliciously hot and creamy and steamy) all on his own and then went off to the Workroom to pick up his tidy-bag. His spirits brightened a bit on the way because, after all, good old Tobermory was *certain* to remember what day it was. Only he didn't.

'Who? Who? Who?' said Tobermory appearing from the back store-room. 'Oh it's *you*, I might have known it. You're a bit on the early side aren't you?'

'Yes,' agreed Bungo in a very bright and eager sort of voice, 'I wanted to get out to work early so that I could get back early you see because it's my . . . my . . . my . . . I say . . .'

'Won't keep you a moment,' said Tobermory trotting into the back store-room. 'Got a little experiment out here and it's not going quite right. Drat! Ouch!'

'Are you all right, Tobermory?' asked Bungo, trying to peer round the doorway.

'Quite all right, thank you,' said Tobermory, reappearing and sucking at one paw. 'Drat! Hot wax, very painful! Ouch! Pick up your tidy-bag young Womble and off you go!'

'Not quite so young really,' said Bungo, 'because today's my . . . oh . . .' His voice ended in a great sigh for Tobermory had once again vanished into the back store-room.

'Nobody cares,' said Bungo to himself, 'Nobody is at all interested that it's my own particular, *special* sort of day. Madame Cholet hasn't remembered because she's too busy with her cooking and Tobermory hasn't remembered because he's too busy with his experimenting. But I'm sure Great Uncle Bulgaria will have remembered. Oh!'

Bungo paused outside Great Uncle Bulgaria's study and read the notice which had been pinned to the door. It said:

'Am *Particularly Busy*. Please Do Not Disturb. Signed, Bulgaria Coburg Womble.'

'Ho hum,' said Bungo, heaving such a big sigh he almost lifted himself off his back paws, and he shuffled off to the main door of the burrow to write his name in the Duty Book and then in the column which was headed 'Tidying Up Area' he put 'as far away as possible'. Because if he was going to feel hard-done-by, he was going to be as hard-done-by as he could be. In fact he very nearly wrote 'so there' in the margin.

As the weather had been quite pleasant recently a great many Human Beings had been out and

about enjoying the Autumn sunshine and, in that
extraordinary way that Human Beings have, they
had left an astonishing amount of litter behind.

' 'straordinary creatures they are,' muttered
Bungo to himself, almost, but not quite, for-
getting his own miseries, 'I mean, fancy throwing
away a nearly full packet of crisps – onion and

vinegar flavour too – and some perfectly good paper-bags, a nearly new scarf, a pair of shoes, three oranges, all these comics, two currant buns (nice and fresh with the dew on them at that), a nylon jacket, half a bar of chocolate, an *unopened* tin of fizzy lemonade and five biros . . . tck, tck, tck! Why, any sensible Womble could be well fed, cosy and entertained for at least three days on this little lot alone. I'll never understand Human Beings, not if I live to be THREE hundred. Oh dear . . .'

And Bungo heaved another enormous sigh, because it had suddenly occurred to him that apparently nobody, no fellow Womble that is, would care *how* long he lived if they couldn't even remember his birthday. He picked up a large carrier-bag from under a bush and decided to fill that up too. If he returned to the burrow with *two* full tidy-bags at least *somebody* might notice how hard he had been working.

However, when Bungo discovered a copy of *The Times* newspaper under a bench his resolve faltered. Not only was it Great Uncle Bulgaria's favourite paper, but it also had the date on it. Bungo suddenly decided that it was time he stopped being dignified and returned to the

burrow and shook everybody's memories up a bit.
He had nearly reached it when he saw Tomsk,
Wellington and Orinoco ahead of him, all of them
very busy turning over what they had tidied up
so far.

'Morning,' said Bungo in a very offhand way.

'Afternoon now,' corrected Wellington, trying

to stuff a very dented old biscuit tin into his tidy-bag.

'That's right,' agreed Tomsk, who was scrabbling about in a great heap of red and green wrapping-up paper which he had gathered together in a kind of small paper mountain.

'Almost *tea-time* actually,' said Orinoco who had a rather sorry-looking yellow tea-cosy in one paw.

'Yes, I daresay,' said Bungo crossly, 'in fact today's already about half over. Today which is a very *special* sort of day, too. I mean look at the date . . .'

Bungo pulled *The Times* newspaper out of his carrier-bag and waved it under their noses.

'So it is,' said Wellington, blinking through his round spectacles, 'you're quite right Bungo, it's . . .'

'It's – what?' demanded Bungo.

'Tuesday,' said Wellington nodding. 'Yes, it says so here at the top. It's Tuesday. I've always thought that Tuesdays are pretty special. There's something about a Tuesday that . . .'

'Apart from *that*, isn't it special?' almost shouted Bungo.

'Don't think so,' rumbled Tomsk holding out his paw. 'Feels a bit like rain to me. I shouldn't be surprised if it rains before nightfall. I shan't be able to play golf if it rains, you know. The ball slides about and you can't get a good grip with your back paws so that . . .'

'On Tuesdays,' said Orinoco dreamily, 'Madame Cholet often gives us acorn pasties with oak-leaf gravy for supper. It's absolutely de-licious and – I say Bungo, where are you off to?'

'The Burrow,' said Bungo heavily. 'I started work early, so Tobermory may,' big sigh, '*may* allow me to finish early. I'd like to finish early today, because it's a very *special* sort of day. Not that it really matters of course . . . Excuse M E!'

And he went off with his nose so much in the air he almost tripped over the front doorstep.

'Hallo, young Womble,' said Tobermory, putting his grey head round the store-room door, 'you're back a bit sharpish. I wonder if, as a great favour, you wouldn't mind doing another half an hour tidying-up duty? The breeze has risen quite a bit and I've had a report that a lot of stuff's been dumped by a coach party to the south-east of the burrow. We don't want it blowing all over the place, do we? Take any carrier-bag you like off the shelf. That's it – yes, I knew I could rely on you Bungo. Excuse me . . .'

And Tobermory vanished before Bungo could so much as open his mouth. Bungo put down his two full tidy-bags, snatched another off the shelf and stumped out. Normally a Womble who was extremely busy and bustling, Bungo felt, for once in his life, that he hardly mattered at all. It was as though his whole tubby little body was shrinking away to nothing. He sighed and sighed, but there was nobody to hear him do it and when he got out into the open there was no sign of his so-called friends Tomsk, Orinoco and Wellington. They appeared to have vanished as completely as Tobermory had done.

'Nobody,' said Bungo in a trembling whisper to the darkening Autumn sky, 'nobody has remembered that it's my *birthday*. My *special* day. The day on which I chose my name Bungo. All right then, I'll go on tidying up the rubbish that's been dumped by Human Beings, I'll do my Duty, I'll fill tidy-bag after tidy-bag and take it back to the burrow. It seems to be all I'm fit for. Oooooo dear . . .'

Poor old (well he *was* older by a whole year) Bungo went on working, pausing now and again to wipe one paw over his eyes. The truth of the matter was that he hadn't felt so small and unimportant since he was in the Womblegarten where of course he hadn't even had a name. So that by the time he returned to the main door of the burrow he wasn't noisy or bustling at all. He no longer thought himself more efficient than Orinoco, nor more clever than Tomsk, nor more worldly-wise than Wellington. He was just a tired, sad, small Womble with his mouth turned right down at the corners.

'I've worked for hours and hours and hours,' whispered Bungo. 'And on my birthday too. My *special* day, oh dear . . .' And he sat down and put his face on his knees and sniffed.

Suddenly the lights in the burrow were switched on and there was the distant, somewhat muffled sound of voices. They were singing.

'Ha-ppy birthday to you. Haaaa-py birthday to you . . .'

Bungo's ears went back and his little round eyes stopped brimming with tears. His fur got all tingly.

'Haaaa-py birthday dear Bun-*go* haaaaaaapy birthday to yoooo.'

'Come inside Bungo, old friend,' said the voice of Orinoco, and Bungo was dragged to his back paws and propelled down the passage and into the Workshop before he could recover his breath.

What a sight met his bedazzled little eyes, for the Workshop had been completely changed! For one thing there were red and green paper streamers suspended from one side to the other, and for another the table had been cleared of bits of this and that and on it were a pile of crackers and a beautiful cake with one wax candle burning away in the centre of it. And round the table

were Great Uncle Bulgaria and Tobermory and
Madame Cholet and Wellington and Tomsk and
Orinoco, all of them wearing red and green paper
hats and smiling like anything.

'I say,' muttered Bungo, 'oh dear, oh me, oh
dear! . . .'

'Happy birthday, Bungo, silly sort of name but
it suits you,' said Great Uncle Bulgaria, 'in a sort
of a way. Well stop gawping, young Womble,
and come and sit down, as I understand there are
one or two small gifts for you, apart from the
particularly splendid cake Madame Cholet has
made . . .'

. 'It's nothing,' said Madame Cholet, smoothing
down her crackling white apron, 'a mere nothing,
although I did have a little trouble with the icing.
However, I think it is now all right, *oui*?'

'Rather,' agreed Bungo, looking at the cake
which was quite smothered in pink holly-berry
icing and which had "Happy Birthday Bungo"
inscribed across the top. It made him feel quite
extraordinarily hungry just to look at it, but somehow he managed to bow to Madame Cholet and
to say in a somewhat squeaky voice.

'*Il est très, très bon, Madame* . . .'

'*Tiens!*' said Madame Cholet shrugging her

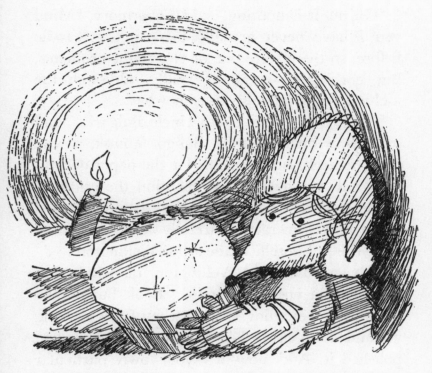

shoulders right up to her silky grey ears, '*Mon petit* Bungo. Ho hum . . .' and she wiped a corner of her spotless white apron across her eyes.

'Then there's the candle,' continued Great Uncle Bulgaria. 'A very splendid candle I'm sure you'll agree, Bungo?'

'The most splendid candle I've ever seen,' agreed Bungo. 'It's smashing! Thank you very much, Tobermory!'

'Oh no, it is nothing,' said Tobermory. 'Mind you I have never actually made a wax candle before, so there were one or two slight problems. But nothing to speak of, really, although the melting down process was somewhat . . .'

'Ah HUM!' said Great Uncle Bulgaria, 'and so to your birthday gifts, Bungo. Tomsk, as you have realized, is responsible for the paper decorations and our hats, not to mention the crackers. Tomsk has never made crackers before so we'd better pull them rather carefully . . . He made all these things himself. While as for Wellington . . .'

'Oh yes, me,' said Wellington, his whole face forming one enormous smile. 'Look Bungo, old friend. It's something I found when I was clearing up and I've cleaned it and un-dented it and polished it. And now it's your own particular treasure box in which you can keep your own particular treasures. There . . .'

It was the rusty old biscuit tin. Only now it looked quite different, because all the dents had vanished and it shone like silver. Indeed it really looked as if it *was* silver as it gleamed in the light of the wax candle.

'I *say*,' said Bungo, in a sniffly sort of voice, 'I say it's ever so . . . that is, oh, goodness gracious me! It's just what I've always *wanted*, Wellington, honestly . . .'

'There's something inside it,' interrupted Orinoco, who for the last five minutes had been shifting about in his chair as he looked first at Bungo and then at that delicious cake.

'Is there?' said Bungo, who by this time didn't know whether he was on his front or his back paws. 'What is it, then?'

'*My* present,' said Orinoco and he leant across the table and opened up the lid of the silvery biscuit tin, and from inside it he produced a newly washed (and still slightly damp) yellow tea-cosy. 'This,' said Orinoco, 'is a very *special* sort of hat. You put it on and pull it over your head and right over your ears, whenever you feel like a special forty winks. You won't hear anything, well hardly anything, when you're wearing this, Bungo. I nearly kept it for myself – well I need a bit of a nap quite often you know – but then I thought it'd make a very special present for you, Bungo old friend, on your *very* special day.'

Bungo couldn't say anything at all. He did try to, but his voice didn't seem to be working particularly well as all it would produce was:

'Th-thank-thank-you-you-you-oh dear . . .'

'And now,' said Great Uncle Bulgaria, getting to his feet and rapping on the table, as he nodded to Bungo who sat down very thankfully and with a thud that made the candle on the cake flicker, 'And now I feel it is time for me to say a few words about our friend Bungo. I have been working on a little speech all day and . . . did you say something Tobermory?'

'Yes,' said Tobermory, 'You can make your speech in a moment or two, Bulgaria, but for the moment I think the most important thing is that Bungo cuts the cake before the candle melts.'

'Hear, *hear*,' said Orinoco.

Tobermory passed a knife across to Bungo, who got to his feet and stood with the knife poised.

'Wish, little one,' said Madame Cholet. 'Make a birthday wish.'

Bungo closed his eyes and wrinkled up his forehead while the other Wombles watched him.

'I wish . . .' said Bungo.

'Silly sort of name, but you get to like it,' murmured Great Uncle Bulgaria.

'I wish,' went on Bungo, 'a very happy birthday to everybody else whose birthday is today. And thank you very, very much all my friends for making this a particularly special day for me. I

didn't think it was going to be a very special day,
but it is. The most special sort of day I've ever had.
Thank you.'

'Happy birthday to you,' Wellington began to sing, and all the others joined in until the burrow was absolutely ringing with the sound.

'I'll make my speech a little later on,' Great Uncle Bulgaria whispered to Tobermory. Tobermory nodded and smiled and then looked at Bungo who was now wearing his yellow tea-cosy with a paper hat on top of it. His round little face was one enormous smile and his little black eyes were sparkling in the light of the wax candle, as he sang,

'. . . happy birthday to meeeeeee . . .'

'Oh dear, oh me, oh my!' said Tobermory, 'it makes you feel quite proud to be a Womble, doesn't it?'

'I,' said Great Uncle Bulgaria Coburg Womble, 'have *always* been proud to be a Womble. The rest of the world couldn't manage without us. And now it's time for my little speech . . .'

'Here we go again,' said Orinoco, nudging Bungo as he helped himself to a third slice of cake.

Slowly and with great dignity Great Uncle Bulgaria got to his feet as the last echoes of 'Happy Birthday to You' rang through the burrow.

'Ah hem, ho HUM!' said Great Uncle Bulgaria . . . 'Bungo Womble, on this, your own very *special* day, I would like to say a few words. First of all – I trust it is a day, the memory of which you will always treasure . . .'

'Oh yes, it I S,' agreed Bungo.

'Good,' said Great Uncle Bulgaria, 'you can

make your speech later, young Womble. But for the moment it's *my* turn . . . As I was saying . . .'

Bungo sat back and folded his paws over his stomach and heaved an enormous (happy) sigh. It's particularly *nice* to feel particularly *special* once in a while.

Don't you agree?

# THE WOMBLES

Elisabeth Beresford

Here they are, the tidy inhabitants of Wimbledon Common whose exploits have delighted readers and TV viewers for years. Meet Great Uncle Bulgaria, the white-furred chief Womble; handyman Tobermory, who turns people's litter into the most amazingly useful things; Tomsk, the golfing Womble; tubby Orinoco, who loves food and forty winks; Madame Cholet, the cook, and last but by no means least, young Bungo, who's just about to go out on the Common alone for the first time...

"A lively, entertaining and humorous book, stuffed with ingenious ideas and endearing characters." *The Times*

"It has its own gentle charm and humour."
*The Times Literary Supplement*

# THE WANDERING WOMBLES

## Elisabeth Beresford

Here they are again, the tidy inhabitants of Wimbledon Common whose exploits have delighted readers and TV viewers for years. When building work threatens the Wombles' burrow, Great Uncle Bulgaria decides it's time to move. Orinoco and Bungo are sent off on a top secret scouting mission to Scotland where they meet the fierce Clan Wombles. Meanwhile, Wellington and Tomsk find themselves exploring the gardens of a Very Important Person indeed!

"Children will enjoy this story wholeheartedly."
*The Junior Bookshelf*

# THE WOMBLES AT WORK

Elisabeth Beresford

The Wombles and their tidying-up exploits have been delighting readers and TV viewers for years. Now living in a burrow under London's Hyde Park, the Wombles face a very difficult problem – pollution! Great Uncle Bulgaria offers a gold medal for the best solution and Bungo, Wellington, Tomsk, Orinoco and all the other Wombles are soon busily at work. Meanwhile, a mysterious stranger looks on...

"A welcome addition to the Womble chronicles, sparkling with fun, crisp in style, endlessly inventive." *The Sunday Times*

"The writing is crisp, the wit genuine and the narrative fast-moving; there is no flagging of inspiration." *The Times Literary Supplement*

# THE WOMBLES TO THE RESCUE

Elisabeth Beresford

The Wombles and their tidying-up exploits have delighted readers and TV viewers for many years. Now they've moved back from Hyde Park to Wimbledon Common, but spirits are low – for the amount of litter has fallen and Womble supplies are shrinking. Great Uncle Bulgaria is called to a crisis meeting in America and Bungo goes with him. So it's left to Tobermory, Wellington, Orinoco, Tomsk and a very odd Womble called Cousin Botany to try and save the day!

"Elisabeth Beresford taught our children to laugh." *Alan Coren*